MW01130208

CARDINALS

ST. LOUIS
ALL-TIME GREATS

BY BRENDAN FLYNN

Copyright © 2021 by Press Room Editions. All rights reserved. No part of this book may be used or reproduced in any manner whatsoever, including internet usage, without written permission from the copyright owner, except in the case of brief quotations embodied in critical articles and reviews.

Book design by Jake Slavik
Cover design by Jake Slavik

Photographs ©: Tom Gannam/AP Images, cover (top), 1 (top), 8; AP Images, cover (bottom), 1 (bottom), 7, 16, 21; Bettmann/Getty Images, 4; Julie Jacobson/AP Images, 9; Transcendental Graphics/Getty Images Sport/Getty Images, 10; Mary Butkus/AP Images, 13; Charlie Riedel/AP Images, 15; Mark Kauffmann/Sports Illustrated/Set Number: X2454/Getty Images, 19; Red Line Editorial, 22

Press Box Books, an imprint of Press Room Editions.

ISBN
978-1-63494-295-9 (library bound)
978-1-63494-313-0 (paperback)
978-1-63494-349-9 (epub)
978-1-63494-331-4 (hosted ebook)

Library of Congress Control Number: 2020913879

Distributed by North Star Editions, Inc.
2297 Waters Drive
Mendota Heights, MN 55120
www.northstareditions.com

Printed in the United States of America
012021

ABOUT THE AUTHOR

Brendan Flynn is a San Francisco resident and an author of numerous children's books. In addition to writing about sports, Flynn also enjoys competing in triathlons, Scrabble tournaments, and chili cook-offs.

TABLE OF CONTENTS

DEAN
17

CHAPTER 1
THE BATTERY

One of the oldest teams in the National League (NL), the St. Louis Cardinals have had their share of big stars. **Dizzy Dean** was the leader of the 1934 "Gashouse Gang" Cardinals that won the World Series. Dean won 30 games that year, the first of four years in a row in which he led the league in strikeouts.

Few pitchers have ever been as dominant as **Bob Gibson** was in 1968. Gibson won the NL Cy Young and Most Valuable Player (MVP) awards. He went 22-9 with 13 shutouts, and his 1.12 earned run average (ERA) that season is a modern record.

The pitcher and catcher together are known as the battery. **Ted Simmons** was a great batterymate for Cardinals pitchers in the 1970s. He also was skilled with the bat. He had the most career hits among all catchers in MLB history when he retired.

Bruce Sutter was not the first full-time reliever in baseball. But he helped usher in the era of a specialized closer to finish games. Sutter was a three-time Reliever of the Year in St. Louis. He tied the MLB record with 45 saves in 1984.

STAT SPOTLIGHT

MOST CAREER PITCHING VICTORIES
CARDINALS TEAM RECORD
Bob Gibson: 251

GIBSON
45

The Cardinals' return to World Series glory in the 2000s was led by two starting pitchers. **Chris Carpenter** won the NL Cy Young Award in 2005. Then he was a key part of the Cardinals' championship teams in 2006 and 2011. Carpenter battled through injuries to become one of the team's most reliable starters.

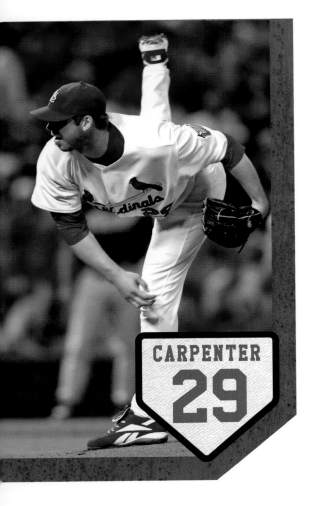

CARPENTER
29

Adam Wainwright began as a reliever, saving the clinching game of the 2006 World Series. He then moved to the rotation and became a three-time All-Star.

MOLINA
4

MASTERMIND

Whitey Herzog built and managed the great Cardinals teams of the 1980s. Herzog served as both manager and general manager in 1981. Early in the 1982 season, he gave up the GM role and managed the Cardinals to the championship. Herzog's teams won 822 games in his 11 years as Cardinals manager.

Yadier Molina was batterymate to both Carpenter and Wainwright. Molina was a great catcher, winning nine Gold Gloves. He also could hit, with a career .281 average through 2020.

HORNSBY
4

CHAPTER 2
IDEAL INFIELDERS

One look at the record books shows the name **Rogers Hornsby** near the top of many hitting categories. The Cardinals second baseman hit .358 for his career. He won seven batting titles, including six in a row from 1920 to 1925, and was named MVP twice. Hornsby had such a good eye at the plate that some umpires believed he knew the strike zone as well as they did.

Albert "Red" Schoendienst had a perfect nickname to play for the Redbirds. The second baseman played 15 years with the Cardinals, making nine All-Star teams.

He then returned as manager in 1965, winning the NL pennant twice. Counting his time as a player, manager, coach, and special assistant, Schoendienst spent a total of 67 seasons with the Cardinals.

Ken Boyer was one of the best third basemen of his era, winning five Gold Gloves in his 11 seasons with the Cardinals. The 1964 NL MVP was also one of the team's best power hitters. His 255 home runs ranked second in team history when he retired. Boyer later managed the Cardinals for parts of three seasons.

STAT SPOTLIGHT

SINGLE-SEASON ON-BASE PERCENTAGE
CARDINALS TEAM RECORD
Rogers Hornsby: .507 (1924)

Shortstop **Ozzie Smith** was a defensive wizard and star of the great 1980s Cardinals. Smith helped boost the Cardinals to the World Series three times in six years. He became famous for his mind-blowing plays in the field.

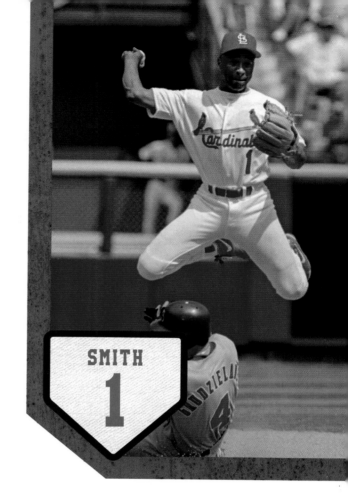

Fans also loved Smith's tradition of doing a backflip while taking the field on Opening Day at Busch Stadium.

Like Smith, **Mark McGwire** also was a huge star in St. Louis. But whereas Smith contributed elite defense, McGwire was all about power at the plate. In his second full season as a Cardinal in 1998, McGwire set a record with 70 home runs. In just 545 games, "Big Mac" slugged 220 home runs. However, his time in St. Louis was tainted by his role in the MLB steroid scandal.

Cardinals fans didn't have to wait long to meet their next great slugger. **Albert Pujols** led the team with 37 home runs in his rookie season of 2001. Pujols never stopped mashing. His 445 home runs in 11 seasons put him second on the team's all-time list.

DAVID FREESE

Infielder **David Freese** played only five seasons in St. Louis. But he'll always be remembered for what he did in the 2011 postseason. The St. Louis native hit .545 with three homers in the NL Championship Series. Then he hit .348 in the World Series, including the game-winning home run in Game 6. Freese was named MVP of both series.

PUJOLS
5

15

MEDWICK
7

CHAPTER 3
PLAYING DEEP

Outfielder **Joe "Ducky" Medwick** once said he wasn't looking to walk. He was at the plate to hit. Medwick did a lot of hitting, winning the triple crown and MVP award in 1937. He also was a key part of the 1934 Gashouse Gang Cardinals.

True to his last name, **Enos Slaughter** destroyed baseballs. He wasn't very kind to pitchers, either. Slaughter was a career .300 hitter and 10-time All-Star. He was known for hustling everywhere he went on the ballfield.

To Cardinals fans, **Stan Musial** is simply "Stan the Man." Musial spent his entire career in St. Louis and holds most of the team's career batting records. A 24-time All-Star and three-time MVP, Musial was one of the greatest all-around hitters in baseball history. He retired with 3,630 hits and 475 home runs.

Curt Flood won seven Gold Gloves while patrolling center field in the 1960s. The three-time All-Star was also known for a lawsuit against MLB that helped create free agency. Flood sued for the right to reject

TONY'S TITLES

Tony La Russa was already a championship manager when he came to St. Louis in 1996. La Russa chose to wear uniform No. 10. It stood for his goal of delivering the Cardinals a 10th World Series title. La Russa built some great teams and finally won that title in 2006. He added another in 2011. He then retired as the winningest manager in team history.

MUSIAL
6

19

being traded. He lost the case, but he helped start a movement to get the rules changed.

Left fielder **Lou Brock** did not have the power of a hitter like Musial. But if Brock hit a single, he was often quickly on second base. Brock stole a record 118 bases in 1974. He led the league in steals eight times and is second on the MLB career list.

Speedy **Willie McGee** was one of the best center fielders of the 1980s. In 1985, he won the batting title with a .353 average. He also stole 56 bases and was the NL MVP. The greatest Cardinals players have contributed

STAT SPOTLIGHT

MOST CAREER STOLEN BASES
CARDINALS TEAM RECORD
Lou Brock: 888

BROCK
20

in a variety of ways. Fans remember all the
parts they've played in 11 World Series titles
and counting.

TIMELINE

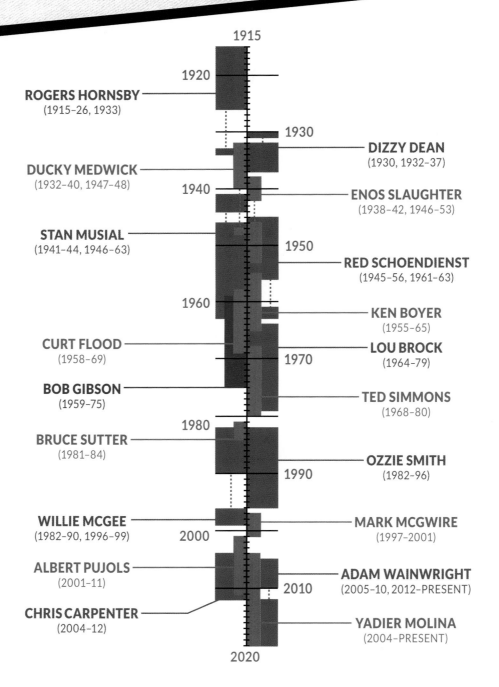

1915

1920

ROGERS HORNSBY
(1915–26, 1933)

1930

DIZZY DEAN
(1930, 1932–37)

DUCKY MEDWICK
(1932–40, 1947–48)

1940

ENOS SLAUGHTER
(1938–42, 1946–53)

STAN MUSIAL
(1941–44, 1946–63)

1950

RED SCHOENDIENST
(1945–56, 1961–63)

1960

KEN BOYER
(1955–65)

CURT FLOOD
(1958–69)

LOU BROCK
(1964–79)

1970

BOB GIBSON
(1959–75)

TED SIMMONS
(1968–80)

1980

BRUCE SUTTER
(1981–84)

OZZIE SMITH
(1982–96)

1990

WILLIE MCGEE
(1982–90, 1996–99)

MARK MCGWIRE
(1997–2001)

2000

ALBERT PUJOLS
(2001–11)

ADAM WAINWRIGHT
(2005–10, 2012–PRESENT)

2010

CHRIS CARPENTER
(2004–12)

YADIER MOLINA
(2004–PRESENT)

2020

ST. LOUIS CARDINALS

Formerly: St. Louis Brown Stockings (1882); Browns (1883–98); Perfectos (1899)

World Series titles: 11 (1926, 1931, 1934, 1942, 1944, 1946, 1964, 1967, 1982, 2006, 2011)*

Key coaches:

Whitey Herzog (1980–90)
822–728 (.530), 1 World Series title

Tony La Russa (1996–2011)
1,408–1,182 (.544), 2 World Series titles

Red Schoendienst (1965–76, 1980, 1990)
1,041–955 (.522), 1 World Series title

MORE INFORMATION

To learn more about the St. Louis Cardinals, go to **pressboxbooks.com/AllAccess**.

These links are routinely monitored and updated to provide the most current information available.

1903 through 2019

GLOSSARY

closer
A pitcher who comes in at the end of the game to secure a win for his team.

Cy Young Award
An award given every year to the best pitcher in the American League and National League.

earned run average (ERA)
A statistic that measures the average number of earned runs that a pitcher gives up per nine innings.

Gold Glove
An award given every year to the top fielder in the league at each position.

triple crown
Leading the league in runs batted in, batting average, and home runs in a season.

INDEX